The Hot Shots

By
Marcie Aboff

Illustrated by
Maurie Manning

CELEBRATION PRESS
Pearson Learning Group

Contents

Saturday in the Park

I was still in my pajamas watching TV, when I suddenly heard a familiar voice behind me.

"I've seen this one. Maniac falls down a mudslide, and Warthog almost drowns in the slime pit trying to save him."

I turned my head and looked back. My best friend, Danny Green, was standing in my living room. Doesn't this guy know Saturday mornings are meant for sleeping late and watching *Maniac Moose and Warthog Will* cartoons?

It was now 9:30 A.M., and Danny is tossing a basketball back and forth between his hands. At least it wasn't 8:30 like last Saturday.

"How'd you get in?" I asked.

"Your mom was leaving for work, so she let me in," Danny said. *Good old Mom*, I thought.

"Come on, Brian, let's shoot some hoops at Central before it gets too crowded," he said.

Danny loves to play basketball. Central is the playground down the street from my apartment. Danny and I have lived in the same apartment building, on the same floor, since we were babies. This year, we're even in the same sixth-grade homeroom at Woodrow Wilson Middle School.

I turned my eyes back to the TV and said, "I know this is a repeat, but it's a good one, and I haven't even eaten yet."

"All right, all right," Danny conceded. He left the room and walked into the kitchen. When he came back, he tossed me a banana. "Here," he said. "Eat, then at 10:00, let's go."

Danny sat down and we watched the rest of the cartoon. It's sort of stupid, but in a cool way. Even my father laughs at Maniac Moose and Warthog Will, but Dad worked late last night and he was still sleeping.

At 10:00, I turned off the TV and went into my bedroom to change. I don't even like basketball that much. I mean it's okay, but I'm not really good at it, especially compared with the athletes at school.

The funny thing is, I grew almost three inches this past year, and I'm now one of the tallest boys in my whole grade. You'd think that would make me a better basketball player, but it doesn't.

My father is good in every sport. I know he wishes I were an athletic kid, and he's always trying to teach me different sports. I played in Little League for a few years, but I struck out more times than I hit the ball, so I quit.

I went back into the kitchen, and Danny was sitting at the table reading the sports section of the newspaper.

"Those Sterlings stink!" he said. "They've lost four out of five games."

"I know, but it's still early in the baseball season," I said. I sat down and poured myself a bowl of cereal and milk, while Danny opened the refrigerator and helped himself to some orange juice.

After I finished breakfast, I wrote my dad a note to let him know I was going to Central. Then I grabbed a basketball out of the hall closet, and we walked outside.

I squinted in the bright sunlight. It was only the beginning of May and we were already having a heat wave. The weather forecast said it might reach 90 degrees by midday.

Danny and I walked down the sidewalk, past other apartment buildings, the grocery store, and the dry cleaner. Central was crowded with mostly little kids on swings and slides and their moms or dads standing behind them or sitting on the benches. I noticed Lorena Martinez pushing her younger sister Lily on the swing.

"Hey, Lor," I said as we passed. She turned around.

"Hi, Brian. Hi, Danny." Lorena is in the sixth grade, also. She lives in the apartment building next to ours. I've known Lorena almost as long as I've known Danny. This year we're both on the Student Council together; she's treasurer and I'm president. Luckily, we can work together and be friends, too.

"Hey, Lorena, come on and shoot some hoops with us," Danny said.

Lorena is good at basketball, even better than most of the boys in our grade. She actually plays all sports—basketball, soccer, softball. She's not full of herself either.

"All right," she said. "Give me a few more minutes with Lily and I'll be there."

There are two basketball courts in the playground, and they were both empty. Danny started dribbling and trying some quick shots. Danny thinks he's going to play for the National Basketball Association when he grows up or at least be a coach.

A few minutes later, Lorena joined us. I tossed her my basketball, and she easily shot the ball into the basket. Danny was trying all these slick moves, missing most of them. If he'd just shoot the ball without all the fancy stuff, he'd probably get more of them in.

I was waiting for Danny to give me a chance with the ball when I saw Jason "Hoops" Cooper and two other seventh-graders strutting toward us. Hoops is the star forward for the Challengers, the Woodrow Wilson Middle School team.

Hoops called out to us, "You guys want to play three-on-three?" Danny looked at me. Danny and I had played two-on-two with the seventh-graders a few weeks ago, and they had slaughtered us. *Did we want to be humiliated again?* I asked myself.

"Sure," Lorena told Hoops.

"Yeah," Danny said, now that Lorena had agreed to play. Danny practiced a fancy shot, but it missed the basket—way missed. The ball landed by the swings.

We laid down the rules—whoever scored 21 first was the winner, one point for each basket. Lorena played against Hoops, and Danny played against Chris. I played against J.D., who is a shrimp of a kid but is lightning quick and really knows how to handle the ball.

J.D. quickly got the ball over Lorena. Chris took the ball up court and shot. *Swoosh!* It went easily into the basket. Lorena took the ball out and dribbled down the court, passing the ball to Danny. Danny dribbled the ball and tried a hook shot, but the ball bounced off the backboard. I went in for the rebound, but Hoops' quick hands snatched the ball away. Hoops ran down the court, shooting the ball in for an easy basket.

"Slammin'!" Hoops said. He slapped hands with J.D. as they passed each other. We played like this

for a little while, and it didn't take long for them to beat us royally, 21 to 8. Lorena scored 5 baskets, Danny got 2, and I got just 1.

Hoops and the other guys grabbed their water bottles and their basketballs. "That was an easy game," Chris said.

J.D. chuckled and looked at us. "Just keep practicing," he said. "When you get older, you'll play better . . . but then we'll be older, too, and we'll still beat the pants off you!"

Hoops and Chris laughed. Hoops snapped his towel at J.D., and they all cackled as they walked away from us.

Danny shook his head and frowned. "They think they're so cool," he said.

I shrugged. "They're good, but you'd think they'd give us a little break once in a while." We all walked over to the water fountain where I took a big drink and splashed some of the water all over my face.

"I'd better go play some more with Lily," Lorena said after drinking some water. "I know she's having fun with Carlos and his mom, but I promised I'd spend the morning with her. See you guys." She waved and walked toward the swings.

Danny took a drink and spit some water on the ground. "Come on, dude," he said to me. "It's you and me, so let's play one-on-one. I've got a new move I want to try out."

I shook my head, feeling really hot. "I'm going to head home," I said. I had had enough basketball for a while. Little did I know that I would soon be neck deep in basketball. When I got to school Monday morning, I found out the real game was just starting.

Students Versus Teachers

A little before lunchtime on Monday, Principal Reese came on the school's speaker system. He called all sixth-graders into the gym for a special announcement.

I slammed my math book closed. *Good*, I thought, I would miss the end of math class. Math used to be my favorite subject, and I've gotten straight As on my report card in math my whole life—until this year. My math teacher, Mr. Trimball, gave me a B last marking period just because I didn't *show* the steps of my work, even though I got most of the answers right!

We walked down the hall and filed onto the gym bleachers. Our gym teacher, Mr. Gesauldo, was holding a microphone and standing next to Principal Reese.

"The annual Sixth-Grade Students versus Teachers Benefit Basketball Game will be held in three weeks," Mr. G. said. "You'll get a chance to battle the teachers on the basketball court, all for a good cause. The proceeds this year will go toward the purchase of new computers for the school." There was some rumbling in the seats.

"Any sixth-grader can sign up," Mr. G. continued, "as long as you're passing all of your subjects. A total of 20 kids can play. If more than 20 of you want to play, we'll randomly pick names from a bowl a half hour before the end of school tomorrow, here in the gym."

"So, if you want to play," Principal Reese said, "sign up on this form that will be taped on the gym wall." He held up a sheet of paper. "We've been playing this fundraising basketball game for four years now, and it's always a lot of fun. Just to let you know—the teachers play to win, and they have won every year." Everyone started to grumble as someone muttered, "Not this year."

As we headed out of the gym, Danny ran up to me. "This will be cool," Danny said. "Let's sign up now."

"I don't think I'm going to sign up," I said.

"What do you mean you're not going to sign up?" Danny asked.

"I'm not a great basketball player," I said as we walked toward the cafeteria for lunch. "I don't want the team to lose."

"You're better than most of the girls."

Was that supposed to make me feel better?

"I heard Jennifer Dalton is signing up and so is Alissa Thomas," Danny said. Then he laughed. "Walter Duncan is signing up, too! I mean who's more clumsy than Walter Duncan?"

I had to grin because Walter is really bad in sports. Whenever we choose teams in gym, he is always the last kid picked. The kid talks so much, he never pays attention to what he's doing. Yet, he's always smiling. *How can anybody be happy all the time?* I thought.

"Come on, you have to sign up!" Danny said as we walked into the cafeteria. The hot lunch was lasagna, and I grabbed some milk to go with it. We sat down at our usual table in the cafeteria. Down at the other end of our table, two of the sixth-grade jocks, Jeffrey Cooper and Kevin Martin, were talking about signing up for the game. Jeffrey is Hoops Cooper's younger brother, and they are both excellent athletes. *That's who should be on the team. Not me*, I thought.

After school, Danny came over to my apartment. My father had just come home from work and was in the kitchen. He's a store manager at Electronic City and works different shifts. That day he got home in the afternoon.

"Hey, guys," he said. "How was school?"

"All right," Danny said. "I can't wait for summer though. Hey, Mr. Chang," Danny continued, "I'm trying to convince Brian to play in the student–teacher benefit basketball game."

Danny told my dad all about the basketball game, and I knew what was coming next. My father looked at me. "You *should* play, Brian," he said. "It would be good experience for you to brush up on your basketball skills."

I rolled my eyes knowing that now I was going to hear it from both of them.

"Listen, I can help you improve," my father said, the excitement building in his voice. "You're not a bad basketball player, Brian. You just need to practice your moves. When I was your age, I played basketball and baseball all the time. Playing sports teaches sportsmanship and cooperation—everyone working together for the sake of the team."

My father turned to Danny. "I was captain of my high school baseball team, did you know that?"

"No, I didn't, Mr. Chang," Danny said.

That's all my father needed to hear. Now he was on a roll. He told Danny about the trophies he had won and how his high school team won the county championship when he was a senior and how he scored two runs to win the final game. Of course, Danny was eating it all up.

"I was good in basketball, too," my father said. My father dribbled an invisible basketball all around the kitchen floor. Then he shot the invisible ball into an invisible hoop.

He cheered. "Two points! Listen, I'll play with you both tomorrow after school. We'll go to the playground and I'll give you some pointers."

"I can't," I told him. "I have a Student Council meeting after school."

"All right," my father said. "Let me see if I can change my work schedule this weekend and we'll practice then."

Great, now Dad was going to change his whole work schedule for this. I groaned to myself.

"Thanks a lot, Mr. Chang!" Danny said. Sometimes I think Danny and I were switched at birth and Danny is really my father's son.

I finally told them both that I would sign up for the basketball game. I only hoped a lot of kids would sign up, and I wouldn't get picked for the first team. At least if I put my name in, Danny would be happy, my father would be happy, and I could get on with my life.

The next day was Tuesday. The kids who had signed up for the game were called into the gym. A total of 32 sixth-graders were there. I tried figuring out the chances of my name being picked—32 signed up, 20 would be chosen. I was looking down at the floor doing the math calculations in my head when I heard my name.

I looked up and saw that Mr. G. had a piece of paper in his hand, and everyone was looking at me. I was the first name picked.

Jeff Cooper's name was called after mine and then a few girls' names. When Danny's name was announced, he looked over in my direction, raised his hand high, and gave me a thumbs-up sign.

Mr. G. read Walter Duncan's name and a lot of kids laughed. "That's me!" Walter shouted. He started jumping up and down in his seat, not seeming to care that everyone was laughing.

Mr. G. read some more names. Then he finally said Lorena's name. Now I knew we had a chance of winning.

After he had read all the names of the kids who would be playing, Mr. G. said, "I bet you'd like to know the names of the teachers you will be playing against. There will be 12 teachers all together. The first one is Mr. Todd."

Mr. Todd, one of the science teachers, is six feet tall. His head looks like a bowling ball because he is bald. I bet he is a decent basketball player.

Mr. G. announced the rest of the teachers. When he mentioned Ms. Walsh, a lot of the boys sighed. She is young and really pretty, but she doesn't look like she'd be such a good basketball player. She doesn't seem like the kind of person who would want to play sports.

Then Mr. G. announced Mr. Trimball, my math teacher. *Short, skinny, Mr. Trimball?* Even the thought of it made me laugh out loud. Now I was getting a little excited. I'd love to play against him; he looks like he would fall on the floor if you just bumped into him.

The last name Mr. G. said was the new English teacher, Mr. Johnson. He is really tall with a big build, and he just *looks* like he'd be an awesome basketball player. Everyone groaned.

When Mr. G. finished reading the teachers' names, he said, "If your name was read, please stay here for a few more minutes. The rest of you please go back to class. You're the lucky ones. You get to watch your fellow classmates lose to the teachers on the basketball court," he laughed.

"The teachers have decided that Mr. Todd will be captain," Mr. G. continued after the other students had left. "They are calling themselves The A Team. You should also decide on a captain and choose a team name. I will be your advisor and will be here in the gym next Thursday afternoon as well as the following Tuesday for you to practice. You might want to organize some practices on your own. You will also need to decide who plays each position."

Then Mr. G. asked who was interested in being captain. Everyone looked around the room, but no hands were raised. I thought Jeff Cooper would raise his hand because he's a great basketball player.

Lorena nudged me. "You be captain!" she whispered. "You were voted Student Council president, so you would get voted for this, too."

I shook my head. "*You* should be captain of the basketball team!" I whispered back. "You're a lot better than me!"

Jennifer Dalton raised her hand. "I'll be captain," she said.

Lorena looked at me. "Now you *really* have to volunteer!" she said. "Jennifer doesn't know a thing about basketball." Before I knew it, Lorena had pushed my elbow up over my head and waved my hand high in the air.

Mr. G. asked me if I was volunteering to be captain or swatting a fly. I swallowed hard. I usually didn't have trouble leading a group. Last fall, I organized the student car wash, and I'm president of the debate team this year. This was different because I had never led a sports team before. Now everybody was staring at me.

For a few seconds, I just sat there like a statue. Then I broke down and nodded yes. So we voted. Jennifer got 6 votes and I got 14. It was the first time in my life that I wished I had lost.

Mr. G. then asked if anyone had suggestions for a team name. "How about the Wizards?" Walter suggested. Walter was into wizardry.

"That's already a *professional* team name," Danny shot back.

"I know a good name!" Jennifer said, fluffing up her long, black hair. "The Radical Ravens." Several girls liked the name, but the boys didn't.

"Oh yes," Danny said, fluffing up his hair. "I'm just *so* radical." The boys all laughed. A few seconds later, the bell rang and we still couldn't think of a name.

Now I really wished our name *was* the Wizards. We were going to have to make things up as we went along, and I wasn't sure I could do it.

Chapter 3

Practice

At dinner that night, I told my dad that I had been picked for the student–teacher basketball game. A huge smile swept across his face, and he slapped his hand on the table. "All right!" he said. "We'll go over some moves tonight."

My mom was also happy for me. "I didn't know you liked basketball that much," she said.

I shrugged. *How could I say anything bad when my dad was so happy?*

"Well," Mom said, "as long as you enjoy yourself and have fun. The money will certainly help the school."

My dad asked who was on the team. I told him there was a total of 12 boys and 8 girls.

"That's a lot of girls," Dad said, "but I guess all of them can't be that bad."

My mom stared at my father. "What do you mean by that, Sam? There are many fine female athletes."

My dad smiled. "I know that, but let's face it. When girls play against girls that's one thing, but when they play with the boys, it's a whole different ballgame."

"Lorena is the best player on the whole team and she's a girl," I told my father. My father looked surprised, and my mother's face broke out in a smug smile.

After dinner, I turned on the computer. If we had any chance of winning I had to do something. I e-mailed Lorena.

Hi, Lorena,

I think we might have a chance to beat the teachers, but we're going to need to practice. I want to organize a few extra practices before the game, and I wanted to know if you would be my co-captain and help me. I want to e-mail everyone on the team and find out when is a good time to practice. Let's get a schedule together. Let me know what you think.

Brian

Lorena e-mailed me back that night and said she'd love to be co-captain. I felt better now. With Lorena's skills and my organization, maybe we would have a chance. We decided on having a practice on Saturday at 10:00 A.M. at Central.

At 9:30 A.M. on Saturday, Danny rang my doorbell. He was wearing a Knicks basketball shirt and another new pair of basketball shoes. That kid must have ten pairs of basketball shoes in his closet. Anytime he gets any extra money or it's his birthday, he buys new shoes.

I looked down at his big feet. "Another pair of shoes?" I asked with no expression in my voice.

These shoes were neon orange with blue and silver trim. Danny lifted up his foot to show me the bottom of his shoe, and I observed the sole of the sneaker was striped with the same colors.

"Cool, huh?" Danny asked. "Now check this out," he said. He unzipped a small compartment on the side of the shoe. Inside the compartment he had some money and a key.

"Great," I said, "and if you ever get lost at night, you could always use the orange lights on your shoes to get home."

Danny smiled. "Good point," he said.

I was ready to go, but then Danny opened his backpack and took out his old basketball shoes. He started unlacing the new orange ones.

"What are you doing now?" I asked.

"I'm not going to wear these *today*! I've got to save them for the big game," Danny said.

When we finally got to Central, Lorena and some of the other kids were already there. Twelve kids showed up all together. "Let's break up into two teams," I said.

Lorena and I put the teams together. I tried having the better players practice against the better players, and the players who weren't so good play against the other kids who weren't so good. I put myself against Jennifer's best friend, Alissa Thomas. Alissa is sort of athletic, and is really good in gymnastics, but I don't think she is such a great basketball player. I guess you could say we are both mediocre.

Jeff started with the ball and passed it to Danny. Danny dribbled up court and shot, but it bounced off the backboard. Jennifer took the ball and dribbled, but Danny stole it back from her.

"Hey!" Jennifer yelled. "I had the ball in my hands. You can't steal the ball like that!"

"Yes, I can," Danny said. "I didn't touch you!"

"It doesn't matter," Jennifer insisted. "I had the ball in my hands and you just grabbed it from me! That's not fair!"

All of us, except for Walter, tried to explain to Jennifer about stealing the ball away. Walter was off in his own world trying to dribble the ball for more than ten seconds without losing control of it.

I had an idea. My father had given me some sheets months ago that listed the basic rules of basketball. I told Lorena about it, then added, "I can make copies and hand them out in school on Monday," I said.

"Great idea, Brian," Lorena said. "You're using your head."

At least, I'm good for something, I thought.

We had started practicing again when Hoops Cooper and Chris walked toward us. "What a crew!" Chris said with his sarcastic grin.

Hoops kept yelling at his brother Jeff, telling him what to do. For a while, Jeff didn't say anything, until he had finally had enough.

"I know what to do!" Jeff insisted.

Hoops held up his hands. "All right, all right, little bro, just trying to help."

Chris laughed. "You guys are going to need help," he said.

"Watch out for Mr. Todd," Hoops continued. "He's tough, and he's got an awesome hook shot."

"He's a really tough teacher, too," Walter chimed in. "When I got a C on my science lab, Mr. Todd made me do the work all over again. I didn't think it was fair and I told my parents, but they told me to keep trying. I finally got most of the answers right and then I ended up with a B. My parents were happy with that."

Everyone looked at Walter, and we shook our heads. The kid blurts out anything.

"You guys didn't even win last year," Danny reminded Chris.

"We would have," Chris insisted, "if J.D. hadn't twisted his ankle." The sixth-graders may have lost last year, but only by four points.

Hoops laughed. "If *we* lost, you guys don't stand a chance," he said. Then Hoops and Chris walked toward the other basketball court.

Walter hollered over toward them, "You think you're such hot shots!"

We ignored Walter and started dribbling the basketballs again. Then I had a thought and told everyone to stop dribbling.

"That's not a bad name!" I said. Everyone looked at me and I could tell no one had any idea what I was talking about.

"Our team name!" I said. "Let's make it The Hot Shots!"

Mostly everyone thought the name was cool, and we decided that would be our team name. I went up to Walter, patted him on the back, and said, "Good job, Walter!"

Walter broke out in a huge smile. "Really? You like it? You like the name Hot Shots? I do, too!" He threw his basketball high in the air. "All right!" he shouted. The ball fell down and bounced back up, nearly hitting Ricky Simon right under his chin.

Ricky had a bad temper and liked to throw his weight around. He had a lot of weight to throw around, too, as he was the biggest kid in the sixth grade. He marched up to Walter and stuck his big face into Walter's face.

"Hey, what do you think you're doing?" he yelled. "The basket's that way! Are you nuts?"

Walter backed off with a scared look on his face, so Danny and I pulled Ricky away. I leaned over to Ricky and whispered, "Leave him alone, Ricky. You know he doesn't know what he's doing."

"Well, he'd better watch it," Ricky said and then he gave a goofy laugh, "or I'll use his head as a basketball!" Ricky can act like an idiot sometimes, but he is a good basketball player, and I didn't want to lose him from the team.

By now, Jeff and Lorena were the only two at the basketball hoop. Jeff was switching directions as he

moved the ball from one hand to the other.

"Hey, Jeff," I said. "You think you could show us how you do that cross-over move?"

"I could try," Jeff said. I called the rest of the team over. Lorena, Danny, and Ricky thought it was easy. Now that Jeff was involved, he spoke up more and tried helping everyone.

We practiced a little while longer until some kids said they were getting tired or hungry and started to leave. I told everyone not to forget practice on

Thursday in the school gym, hoping that they would *show up* at the next practice.

Danny, Lorena, and I walked home together. We stopped at the grocery store for something to drink. I got a bottle of water and Danny headed for the sports drinks.

"Hey, you guys, check this out," he said.

Next to the usual sports drinks, there was a new brand called 'ZING' with pictures of different sports figures on the bottle. Danny read us what the bottle said.

"Get some ZING! ZING will give you the edge. Our unique combination of fluids will supply energy and power like no other sports drink can. It tastes great, too! So, beat the competition! If you want to win, get ZING!"

"Sounds good, huh?" Danny asked.

"They're just trying to get you to buy the drink!" Lorena said. "It's probably the same as all the other sports drinks."

I agreed with Lorena, but I still grabbed the Knock-Out Punch flavor. I would try anything that might help us out. Danny got the Grand Slam Blueberry and we went to the checkout counter.

At the end of the line, Lorena came over with the ZING's Nothin'-But-Net Nectarine. She grinned.

"Nectarine is my favorite flavor!" she insisted.

Chapter **4**

Spying on the Teachers

The next week there were posters about the game all over the school. The local newspaper's banner headline read, *"Watch Students and Teachers Battle on the Basketball Court!"* The big buzz around school was that this year for the first time, Channel 68, the local cable station, was going to tape the game and broadcast it on TV.

On Tuesday in English class, Jennifer told Alissa that she was going to be the next star of the WNBA, the Women's National Basketball Association. "If I mess up at the basketball game," she said as she fluffed up her hair, "I'll just start singing for the cameras, and a record producer will discover me and offer me a recording contract!" She giggled.

"I'll start doing back flips," Alissa said. "Someone from the Olympic committee will be sure to see me and want to coach me, and I'll get a gold medal at the next Olympic games!" They both laughed.

Great, I thought as I listened. *They really don't care about winning the game.*

Danny told me how good it was that he got his new orange basketball shoes. "The camera will be following my every move!" he declared.

So everyone was more excited about the TV station than the game while I was just feeling more nervous. Now the TV station would show the game to even more people. I could just hear the announcer, *"Teachers beat students by landslide! Biggest point spread since they first started playing the benefit game."*

After school, Danny, Lorena, and I were walking home when Danny said, "Too bad we can't see the teachers in action."

"What do you mean?" I asked.

"You know—watch them. Check out their strategies, their moves, and see who really is a good player and who we have to watch out for."

"That might not be so hard to do," Lorena said as she looked at me. "The teachers are practicing tomorrow after school, right?"

"That's what I heard," I said.

"They'll be practicing in the gym and the gym has windows. If we just *happen* to pass by, we can't help but see what's going on."

"Yes," Danny said. "If we hide behind the bushes at the back windows of the gym, they'll never even see us."

"Are you in, Brian?" Danny asked.

"Listen to you!" I said. "Don't you have any confidence in us? Don't you think we have a chance of winning without spying on the teachers?"

Danny and Lorena looked at each other. "No," they both said at the same time. They weren't kidding.

"All right," I said. "Let's try."

The next day after school, Danny, Lorena, and I waited outside, behind the building. We kept our backs to the building as we crept toward the gym windows. I could hear the pounding of basketballs and the squeaking of sneakers across the smooth gym floor.

We crouched behind the bushes in front of the gym windows. Flies were darting in and out of the shrubs. It was hot and all the gym windows were open. Now we'd have to be really quiet, too.

I lifted my head a little to see who was in the gym. I saw Mr. Todd shooting the basketball and dribbling with a lot of control. He is big all over, big arms and legs, making him look more like a wrestler than a basketball player.

Ms. Walsh was there, too. She was even wearing knee guards. She had her long blonde hair tied back in a ponytail, and she was shooting the ball pretty well. Surprisingly, she attacked the ball and jumped up for a rebound.

The new teacher, Mr. Johnson, was just walking into the gym with Ms. Bailey, the school librarian. Ms. Bailey is really old, and she always wears these old-fashioned dresses tied up to her neck. Everyone in school jokes that when the school was built over a hundred years ago, Ms. Bailey must have been one of the first teachers. It was funny to see her in shorts and a T-shirt.

I was hoping Mr. Trimball would be there. Now *that* would be a riot! I could see him attempting to run across a basketball court as I imagined his legs looking thin and bony.

I remembered last week in his class, when he was

handing back a really hard math test.

"We have a few A's on the test, ladies and gentlemen," Mr. Trimball said. "Ms. Hollis, Mr. Goldstein, and Mr. Chang all got A's." I had smiled to myself.

Mr. Trimball walked by everyone's desk and handed the tests back. As he walked by my desk he showed me my test, but when I held out my hand to take it, he grabbed the paper back.

He looked around the room and raised his voice. "Except Mr. Chang will end up with a B," Mr. Trimball announced. "Mr. Chang did not show his work when the instructions said explicitly to *show* your work. This is the second time you've done this Mr. Chang. Next time, read ALL the instructions and organize your work, or you might fail, no matter how well you do on the test." Then he turned the paper over on my desk.

The guy was out to get me, I just knew it. I couldn't wait to get him on the basketball court.

Danny bumped against me. "Ow!" he said, "These shrubs are prickly."

Lorena wiped her legs. "I know," she agreed.

"Sshh," I told them. "Somebody is going to hear you."

"Move over," Danny said to me. "I can't see all the teachers."

Still bending down, I inched over and then Lorena moved over, too. When Danny moved over, he lost his footing and fell down on his knees with a hard thump.

"EEEOOOOOWWW!" Danny screamed.

It couldn't hurt that much, I thought. All the teachers turned to look out the window. Danny was holding his knee, and when I looked at him I saw a bee's stinger sticking out of his right knee.

A few of the the teachers gathered around the window, while Mr. Todd and some of the other teachers came running outside. By this time, Danny's knee was turning red and swelling up. There was a bee lying flat on the ground, its wings fluttering underneath him.

"It looks like you crushed him," Mr. Todd said as he scraped the stinger from Danny's knee.

"Who cares about the stupid bug?" Danny cried. "I'm the one in pain!"

"Now, Danny," Mr. Todd said, helping him up. "He just stung you, but you practically crushed him to death. Are you allergic to bee stings?"

"Good and no," Danny said, holding his knee.

"Let's get you into the nurse's office anyway," Mr. Todd said. He slung Danny's arm around his shoulder and helped him walk toward the nurse's office.

The nurse wasn't in her office, so Mr. Todd cleansed the wound with soap and water. Then he took out an ice pack and held it on Danny's knee.

Mr. Todd raised his eyebrows and asked us, "What are the three of you still doing here, anyway? I didn't know you liked school so much."

We looked at each other and didn't say anything until Lorena finally told him, "We were working on a science project."

Then Danny hopped on board. "Yeah," Danny added. "We're studying local vegetation in Ms. Harkins' class."

"How convenient," Mr. Todd said in a completely skeptical voice.

After a few minutes, Mr. Todd put some antiseptic on a cotton ball and wiped Danny's knee. Danny grimaced.

"I think you'll live," Mr. Todd told Danny. He carefully placed a bandage on Danny's knee. "If you're still in pain later tonight or the swelling increases, make sure you go to the doctor," Mr. Todd said. Danny nodded.

"I'm so happy the three of you are such conscientious students," Mr. Todd continued, "and I truly admire the dedication to your schoolwork. If I were you, I might practice more for the big basketball game. You know it's only a week and a half away, and we've got an amazing team."

Of course, Mr. Todd didn't believe a word we were saying about the vegetation. He knew we had been spying on the teachers, but he didn't say so.

Mr. Todd grinned. "Now why don't the three of you go home, do your homework, and then practice some basketball? The teachers would like a little competition this year."

Lorena and I walked home as Danny hobbled beside us. Danny's knee was fine by the next day, and I decided that spying on the teachers wouldn't help us anyway. Neither would drinking ZING. It didn't make me any stronger, and I didn't even like the taste. We needed a new strategy—*right away!*

Chapter 5

The Fight

The next morning I reminded everyone on The Hot Shots team about practice that afternoon in the school gym.

"I can't go," Alissa said. "I have cheerleading."

"What time does it start?" I asked.

"4:30."

"Well, you can come for the first half-hour," I said. "We need you!"

Alissa smiled and said she would try. Some other kids had excuses, too. Jeff said he had two big tests the next day and had to study. Jennifer said she had a haircut appointment, but she would try to reschedule for later. I tried to convince everyone we needed to practice if we were ever going to win.

Sixteen kids showed up to practice. Mr. G. suggested we start out with some basketball drills like three man weave and lay-up lines. Then we started a scrimmage. Whenever Ricky had the ball, he never passed it, he just shot.

"Stop being a ball hog," Danny said to him.

"Yeah!" Walter added, but when he saw Ricky's angry face, he sped out of the gym. "Gotta go to the bathroom!" he called back to us.

"One person can't carry a team," Mr. G. said. "You have to play together if you're going to win." *He has a good point*, I thought as I nodded.

Ricky grumbled to us. "Fat chance the way this crew is playing." He whipped the ball to Lorena. I thought Ricky would pack up and leave, but he stayed for the rest of the practice.

The next Saturday morning, my father was dressed in shorts and a basketball shirt when I went down to breakfast. He whistled as he made the two of us pancakes. When Dad whistles, he's in a good mood. He was taking Danny and me to Central that morning to practice.

As we walked to the playground, my father said, "You know, you need good basketball skills to win the game, but basketball is a mental game, too."

"What do you mean, Mr. Chang?" Danny asked.

"You have to believe in yourself. If you don't think you're going to make the basket, you're not going to."

Danny and I looked at each other. I rolled my eyes and Danny grinned. That was pretty basic, and this sounded like the beginning of a lecture.

"It's good to block out all distractions and just focus on the game," my father said. "When you're shooting, believe the ball is going to go in and you'll have a better chance of scoring."

"Oh, I believe," I said. "I can believe until I'm 150 years old, but I don't think that's going to help me score."

"I'm talking about confidence, Brian. Being positive is important. Not everyone is going to play like Michael Jordan."

When we got to Central, my father dribbled the ball to the basket and jumped high in the air. The ball hit the backboard and fell into the hoop. He dribbled again, turned completely around, and shot again, but the ball hit the rim and bounced down. Danny grabbed it, dribbled to the other basket, and shot the ball in.

My father took the ball. "All right. Before we play, we have to warm up. Let's stretch out our muscles. You need flexibility to be a good basketball player."

Danny and I watched my father as he bent to the ground. "Stretch out your calves," my father said. "Let's go," he commanded us. "One, two, three, stretch out your legs."

We followed him. Then he clasped his hands together and held them high over his head. "Stretch out your arms," he continued. I felt like I was in gym class. I looked around the playground, hoping I wouldn't see anybody I knew because I felt silly waving my arms in the air.

My father stood up and shook out his arms and legs. "Ankle roll!" my father announced.

"What?" Danny and I both asked.

"Ankle roll helps avoid sprains. You walk on all sides of your feet," my father said. "Watch me."

I watched Dad in disbelief. He rolled his ankles to the outside and walked on the outside of his foot. Then he rolled his ankles to the inside and walked on the inside of his foot. He walked on his toes and finished by walking on his heels. "Let's go, gentlemen," my father ordered. He was never in the army, so I didn't know why he was acting like a drill sergeant.

"Don't be embarrassed, "my father insisted. "The pros do this all the time."

Danny and I cracked up. We tried to follow my father, but I felt totally spastic and stupid. When it came time to walk on our toes, Danny quit. "I don't think so!" he declared. "I'm not a ballerina!"

My father gave in. "All right, all right," he said as he winked at us. "When you guys reach the NBA, you'll remember I taught you these warm-ups, and you'll thank me."

"Sure thing, Dad," I said. Then we finally got to play. My father watched Danny and me with a close eye, giving us pointers as we played.

"Dribble lower so you won't get the ball stolen from you, Brian," he kept telling me. "Danny, keep your elbows in when you shoot."

My dad went on. "See your man *and* the basketball," he said. "You need to be able to see your man and help your teammates at the same time. When on offense, make sure your team gets a shot every time. On defense, contest every shot the other team makes."

We had a pretty good practice, but I think my father was having the best time of all.

"All right," he said after almost an hour and a half. "I have to go home, shower, and run some errands, but you two can stay and practice."

I thanked my father for helping us, and he gave me a big smile. "No problem," he said. "Both of you are doing great; just keep practicing." He walked out of the playground, and Danny and I kept playing. Danny grabbed the ball and tried another fancy shot from almost mid-court.

"What are you doing?" I yelled.

"I wanted to try for a three pointer," he yelled back.

I walked up to him. "You know, if you would just shoot the ball without trying to show off, you'd score more baskets," I told him.

Danny put his hands on his hips, "How do *you* know everything?" he shot back. "I've been playing basketball my whole life!"

"Don't get so bent out of shape," I said. "I don't know everything. I was just trying to help. I think we would score more points if we focused on the fundamentals. I want to win this game!"

"I want to win this game, too!" Danny said. "You have to try different strategies, take a chance, make a fake. You wouldn't know that because *you* were never on a real basketball team, and here you are captain." Danny shook his head and mumbled, "Amazing!"

I didn't say anything. What was I doing being captain of a *basketball* team? I was just an average player at best. Now I was fighting with my best friend over a game.

Danny grabbed his towel and started walking off the court. "I have to go," he said under his breath.

I watched him leave. Danny and I have had our fights before but not about basketball. Still, I wasn't about to run after him because I knew it wouldn't change anything. I stayed a little while longer, practicing some lay-ups, jump shots, and hook shots. Some of the balls went in. Some didn't.

As I walked home alone, I could just see the announcer on cable TV. *"Brian Chang and the rest of The Hot Shots were buried by the teachers on Friday night. The teachers massacred the students in their easiest benefit basketball game in years."*

On Monday morning, Danny and I walked to school together like we usually did. We talked like we normally did, and neither of us mentioned Saturday at the playground. That's what usually happens when Danny and I fight. We both need time to cool off away from each other.

Monday night my father surprised me and came home from work early to practice with me. He told me my skills were improving, and I felt like I was playing better, too. I *was* scoring more baskets, but I still knew I wasn't that great.

Tuesday after school, the team practiced in the gym. We stretched out for five minutes and performed

some drills before we broke up to play a game.
Mr. G. said we were doing better.

I wrote Lorena an e-mail later that night.

Hey, Lorena,

I'd like to have one more practice at Central before the game on Friday. Is Thursday good for you? Mr. G. said it would be okay. I also have some ideas on how to separate everyone on the team in groups of five—one group for each quarter. I could really use your help with this.

Thanks, Brian

We had a good turnout for our last practice on Thursday, with only three players who couldn't make it. It finally looked like The Hot Shots were playing more like a team. In my group, Jennifer took the ball and made a crisp two-handed pass to Jeff. Jeff took the ball, made a fake like he was going to shoot, and then passed the ball to me. Ricky was guarding me, but I stepped to the right, snared the ball, aimed, and shot. *Swish!* It went off the backboard and into the basket.

Lorena said her group played a pretty good game, too. She said even Walter scored a basket.

Mr. G. worked with us to make the final list of who would be playing each quarter. "This was a good idea," he said to me as we handed copies to everyone. "This way everyone gets to play."

I decided Danny and I should play in the same quarter. We had played so much basketball together that we knew how each of us handled the ball. He wasn't too happy that Walter would be playing with us, but I reminded him that we were a team.

Before the team left for the night, Mr. G. told everyone how much he thought we'd improved. The team gathered around, and we stacked our hands one on top of the other. "On the count of three," I said. "Who's going to win? One, two, three . . ."

"The Hot Shots!" we all yelled.

Did we really stand a chance? I wondered.

Chapter 6

The Big Game

Finally, Friday was here. My mom made spaghetti for dinner because Dad said carbohydrates are good to eat before a game; they give you energy. I ate as quickly as I could, but I was too nervous to enjoy it. My father was giving me some last minute basketball tips, and my mom showed me the big sign she had made that said LET'S GO HOT SHOTS!

I put on my gym shorts and my new white T-shirt with navy blue writing that said *Hot Shots*. All the kids on the team had been given a shirt with their own names and numbers on the back. The teachers would be wearing navy blue shirts with white letters that said *A Team*.

When we got to the gym, rows and rows of bleachers were pulled out as far as they could go onto the floor. I saw Hoops, J.D., and Chris with some other seventh-graders at the very top of the bleachers.

Danny, his mom, and his younger sister were standing in front of the bleachers. Danny was wearing his neon orange basketball shoes. My parents walked up to Danny's mom and started talking.

Danny gave me a sly smile. "You ready?" he asked.

"Sure," I said, imitating my father. "Just remember, if you think the ball will go in the basket, the ball will go in the basket." We laughed, wishing it were so easy.

On one side of the gym, some kids from the school band were playing sport songs. On the other side of the gym, the TV crew from Channel 68 was setting up. Some guy was holding a tall, bright light near the camera operator, while the Channel 68 news reporter held a microphone in her hand. A lot of kids were hanging out by the camera, watching them set up. Jennifer and Alissa were waving and dancing.

I saw Mr. Trimball walk into the gym. He looked skinny when he was teaching, but now in his T-shirt and basketball shorts, he looked like a beanpole with a head attached.

At 8:00 P.M., Mr. G. took the microphone, and a hush fell over the huge crowd. He welcomed everyone to the Fifth Annual Students Versus Teachers Benefit Basketball Game, and the crowd applauded. Mr. G. announced our team and called out our names one by one. The crowd clapped and cheered for each of us. When mom stood up and lifted her poster high over her head, I felt excited and nervous at the same time. Then Mr. G. announced all the teachers.

Before the teams got into position, our whole team stood up and we put our hands together. "On three," I said. "One, two, three . . ."

"HOT SHOTS!" we all yelled.

The first-quarter players got into position. Jeff Cooper and Ms. Walsh stood in the middle of the court for the tip-off. They were both about the same height. The referee tossed the ball, and the game had finally begun.

Ms. Walsh jumped high and slapped the ball right to one of the other teachers, Ms. Lopez. She brought the ball up court and passed it to Mr. Todd, who drove it to the basket for a quick lay-up.

49

Alissa took the ball and brought it down court. She passed it to another player who caught the ball at the foul line. He made a fake move, then dribbled toward the basket for the shot. Ms. Walsh jumped high in the air and slammed the ball down.

How did she do that? You'd never guess by looking at her how good she is. My stomach dropped as I thought, *This was going to be a very long game.*

Mr. Todd had the ball and slowly dribbled to his basket, scoping out the defense on the court. Weaving in and out between Alissa and Jeff, Mr. Todd broke in for a hook shot. The score was A Team, 4—Hot Shots, 0, and we had played less than two minutes.

By the end of the first quarter, the score was A Team, 16—Hot Shots, 8. Jeff ended up scoring three baskets and Alissa scored one. We had some serious catching up to do. Lorena was playing in the second quarter, and she was our best shot at chipping away at the lead.

Lorena started with the ball and dribbled to the basket. She passed the ball to a teammate, then ran under the hoop. The ball was passed back to her, then she leaped high and sunk the shot.

The new teacher, Mr. Johnson, took the ball down court with an awkward, high dribble. Walter ran right up next to him and stole the ball away!

Clutching the ball, Walter quickly looked to the left, then to the right. He stood frozen in place.

"Pass the ball!" Danny yelled.

Lorena broke herself free from a defender, and Walter finally passed the ball to her. Everyone on the bench cheered.

Lorena dribbled down court and made another basket. One of the teachers took the ball and passed it to Mr. Johnson. Mr. Johnson dribbled to his basket and shot. It was an air ball, not even close. I was really surprised. This big, athletic-looking guy was a worse basketball player than I was.

Lucky for us, Lorena had her usual spark and we gained some much needed points. At half-time, the score was A Team, 28—Hot Shots, 26.

In the locker room at half-time, we were all pumped up. We were really in the game and the pressure was on! Mr. G. led us in a cheer.

In the beginning of the third quarter, Mr. Trimball walked onto the court. Now *this* would be funny. I sat back in the chair ready to laugh.

The next thing I saw I couldn't believe. Mr. Trimball took control of the ball and flew down the court like a professional player. He dribbled the ball between his legs and behind his back, then turned around and flew by our defense. He faked to Ms. Bailey, coasted by Ricky Simon, and shot a three pointer! My eyes bugged out—this couldn't be the same teacher!

Ricky was playing all over the court, barely passing to any of our teammates. After Mr. Trimball scored again, Ricky grabbed the ball and ran straight toward our basket. *Crash!* He fell over Ms. Bailey's feet and slid across the floor like a penguin on ice!

The referee blew the whistle as Mr. G. ran to Ricky and helped him up. Ricky said he still wanted to play. After three quarters, the score was A Team, 39—Hot Shots, 34. There was only one more quarter to catch up. I'd be playing in that one, but I wasn't confident that I'd be much help.

Danny bounced the ball from the base line. He was cornered near the basket when he saw Jennifer open on the left. He passed her the ball and she banked in the jump shot.

"Nice shot," I said. She flipped up her hair and smiled. "Thanks," she said.

The teachers missed an opportunity to score, and Danny ran with the ball down court. He tried a fancy hook shot and missed, but he got the rebound, and this time he scored.

The clock was ticking away. One of the teachers fouled twice and we were catching up. Jennifer passed the ball to me and I dribbled to the basket

and shot. It bounced off the rim and into the basket. Another player on our team made some surprisingly good shots, hustling throughout the quarter to score six points.

One minute to go, and the score was A Team, 49—Hot Shots, 48. With only ten seconds left, I had the ball in my hands. I had faked a pass to Jennifer on my left when I saw Danny out in the open behind her. I flung the ball to him, he caught it, dribbling it once. He aimed and shot over Mr. Trimball's head. It was an easy, straightforward jump shot—*Swish— nothin' but net!*

The buzzer rang, and I raised my hands high. The final score was A Team, 49—Hot Shots, 50!

We went wild! Danny ran up to me and threw his arms around me. "Is this the sweetest win or what?" he cried.

The band jammed "Celebration," and the crowd roared and stomped their feet.

"Great shot!" I said to Danny.

"Great pass!" Danny said to me.

I put my arm around Lorena's shoulder. "You carried us, Lor! Did you get 8 points or 10?" Lorena smiled. "I made 12, but who's counting?"

The next thing I knew, my father and mother were out on the floor. My father was beaming as he patted my back. "Great game, captain!" he said.

"I only scored one basket," I said.

My father smiled. "That's all right, Brian. You made the assist. Plus you organized the whole team, which is the hardest job of all!"

When he said this, it made me realize that I didn't have to be the greatest player. I really was a fairly good leader, and now I knew that was important.

Walter was running around chanting, *"Hot Shots rule, Hot Shots rule!"* Then the rest of us joined in.

When we walked back into the boys' locker room, we passed by the group of seventh-graders.

"Good game, Jeff," Hoops said to his brother.

"Not bad for sixth-graders," Chris added.

J.D. didn't say anything. He just looked down at the floor. "Cool shoes," he told Danny.

The next night, the teachers took The Hot Shots out for a pizza dinner to celebrate. We were still flying high from our win.

Mr. G. told us the game raised more than $1,500 for new computer equipment for the school. That was the most money they had raised in the five years they had played the benefit game.

"I have to hand it to you guys, you really surprised us," added Mr. Todd. "I think I speak for the rest of the teachers when I say this was our most exciting game ever. You never gave up and really pulled it together, especially at the end."

The waiter brought the pizzas to the table and we all dug in. Mr. Trimball came up to me.

"Nice work, Mr. Chang," he said. "You showed you have the stuff to be a good captain. Now just *show* that kind of organization and determination on your math papers and you'll ace my class."

I had to smile because I had to admit he was right. "You were pretty good out there yourself," I said.

"I know, I surprise a lot of people. Nobody would guess from looking at me that I can play basketball. You should see me play ice hockey!"

We laughed and ate our pizza. Never again would I judge people on how they looked.

"Next stop, the NBA!" Danny declared.

Across the table, Mr. Todd asked, "How about going to high school first?"

"Not a bad idea," Danny said. "I could play in a student–teacher basketball game in high school." He raised his arms and nearly shouted, "We'll beat the high school teachers in that game, too!"

I looked at him. *"We?"*

"Sure," Danny said. "Why not?"

I shrugged, then I smiled. Right then, I couldn't think of any reason why I couldn't play in that basketball game, too. In the near future, though, I thought I'd take it easy for a while. After all, I had more than two years to practice!